W9-BBH-060

A Boy With A Cape

The true story about the superhero in all of us

Written by
Amy Logan

Illustrated by
Rich Green

Published by
Full Heart Publishing, Full Heart LLC
Printed in USA, copyright © 2016. All rights reserved.
No part of this book may be reproduced in whole or in part,
without written permission from the publisher or author.
Title fonts courtesy of *Fontscafe.com*.

First Edition, First Print
ISBN-13: 978-0-9890465-4-1

Get additional books and capes at:

GotYourCape.com

Can someone so small make a difference at all?
Can someone like you make the world seem brand new?
I'm not sure you know this, but I tell you it's true.
It's a story of a superhero, of a kid just like you.

So get ready, get set, and let's jump right in...

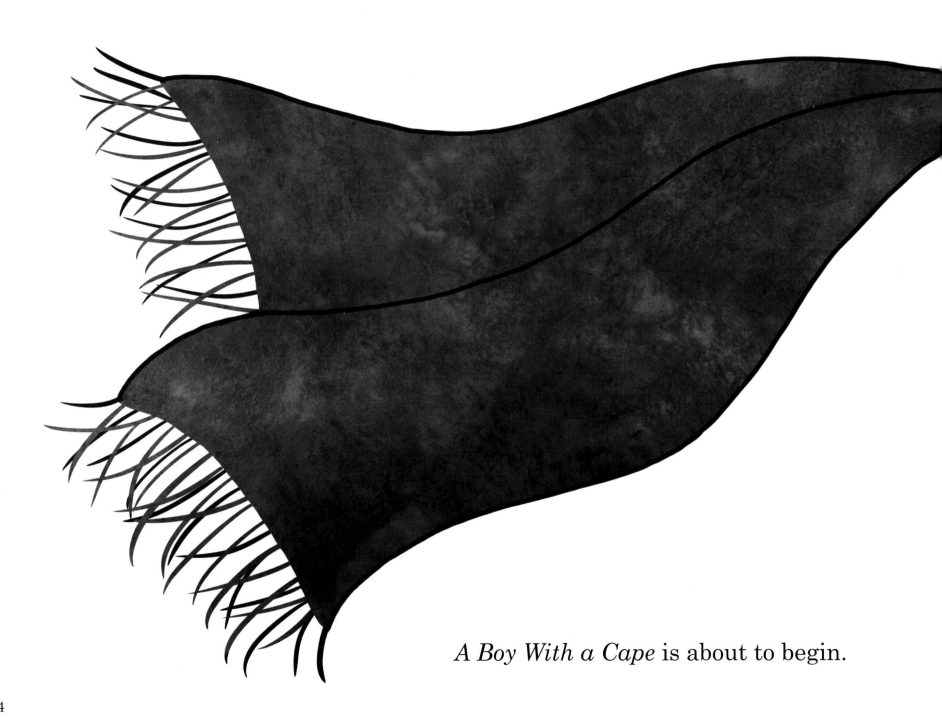

A Boy With a Cape is about to begin.

4

Once upon a time, there was a boy with a cape.

Well not *really* a cape, but a scarf that he tied,
but it *felt* like a cape because he felt SUPER inside.

The boy felt something
so strong in his mind.
He could change the world
in a matter of time.
Not sure what to do,
he just knew, *"There's more..."*

which is why every day the cape he wore.

8

Want to know what happened on Saturday?

On Saturday, he woke up refreshed and bright-eyed.
Ready to go, the cape he tied.
Brushed his teeth, ate his breakfast, his day ready to start...

then said, "*Mom, I love you…with all of my heart.*"

Now, what he **didn't** realize is
mom worked pretty hard.
She was tired from yesterday
weeding the yard.
Mom was **so** tired, all she
wanted was bed,

but the **_I LOVE YOU_** filled mom's heart, so she did this instead:

She made the bed.
She vacuumed the floor.
She planned a dinner then went to the store.
She called a friend
she missed a bunch.
They got together and had some lunch.
She was nice to the server
who wanted to quit.
She complimented her and gave a big tip.
The server worked harder
because she was grateful.
People waited in line to eat at her table.
She earned an award because she was great...

14

all from the "*I love you*" from the boy with the cape.

On Sunday, the day started just like the last;
a high-five and kind word to mom as he passed.

"Love you, too, Mr. Man!"

"Love you, Mom!"

16

The boy went out searching for
something SO GRAND.
To make the world BETTER is
what he had planned;
something SO BIG that would
make him feel TALL;
to make a BIG DIFFERENCE
from a boy so small,

because although he was little, he knew there was more,
and in case Sunday was the day, the tied cape he wore.

Do you want to hear more of what he had in store?

On Monday, he helped with the recycling bin.
He cheered on his favorite team for a win.
He stood up for a kid who was bullied in class.
He helped with the shopping and pumping the gas.
He said "*Please*" and "*Thank You*" and "*That's a cool hat*"
and all of a sudden, no sooner than that…

the kind words didn't stop — they continued to go on.
They traveled to the next guy,

the next one,

and so on...

"I've got your back."

"You're a great teacher."

"I'm so glad we spent the day together."

"I made these for you."

"Let's shoot some hoops."

"You're an awesome singer!"

BUT...

He didn't see any of this magic take place.
To him, it was normal to put a smile on a face.

So...

On Tuesday, he started to question the cape!

"HEY CAPE! What difference do YOU make?
I still have no powers! I'm no superhero!
What have I done? That's a big fat zero!
Nothing I tell you! Nothing at all!
I can't make a difference! I'm just way too small!"

Just then, mom came in to settle him down.
His sadness was sad, a big old sad frown.

Mom said,
"*I heard what you said,*
and it's not even true.
The world is much **better**
and it's **because** *of you…*

Look!
The recycling is out and it's ready to go.
Your favorite team won, they put on quite a show!
The kid who got bullied gets bullied no more.
You made people laugh while you helped at the store.
The gas tank is full, son, I wish you could see...

...yourself through my eyes. What a sight that would be!

And do you want to know something else that I know?

What you do matters everywhere that you go.

It just takes a little to do quite a lot,
and you **are** a superhero though you think you are not.
A superhero's job is to do good each day;
to help others and be kind in every which way.
And you, Mr. Man, do that all of the time
and I want you to know,
I'm so glad that you're mine.

The best I can tell you,
I hope you can see
that you matter to others...

   ...and you matter to me.

I think you're the biggest difference maker of all.
You may think you're small,
but your words make you tall.

Your heart, and your smile,
you don't need a cape.
Your actions and kindness,
those *things make you great!*

So, now that you know that your powers are true...

tell me superhero...

what next will you do?"